PUZZLE ISLAND

Susannah Leigh

Illustrated by Brenda Haw

Designed by Kim Blundell

Contents

Additional designs by Brenda Haw

Series Editor: Gaby Waters

About this book

This book is about a young pirate called Sam Swashbuckle, his pet parrot, Percy, and their adventures on Puzzle Island.

Sam's new boat

Percy the parrot

Useful equipment

Sam Swashbuckle

Sam is a junior pirate. To become a real pirate, he has to find a skull and crossbones badge, like the one shown on the left. The badge is hidden in a chest full of treasure and buried somewhere on Puzzle Island. An exciting trail of clues and puzzles will lead Sam to it.

Skull and crossbones badge

Puzzle Island

Treasure chest

You will find a puzzle on every double page. See if you can solve them all and help Sam to follow the treasure trail. If you get stuck, you can look at the answers on pages 31 and 32.

2

The Pirate Kit

On his journey, Sam also collects a pirate kit. One piece of kit is hidden on every double page. See if you can spot the pieces as you go. If you can't find them all, the answers on page 32 should help you. Here you can see the complete pirate kit.

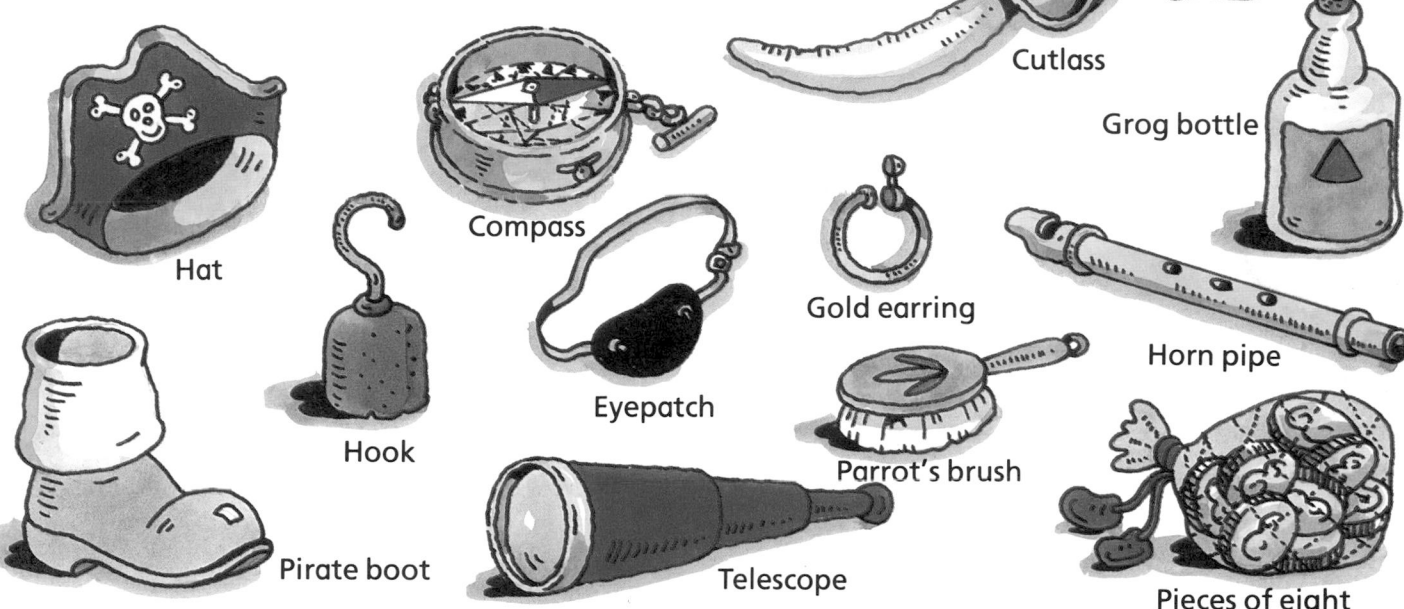

Spare headscarf

Be, careful!

Cutlass

Grog bottle

Hat

Compass

Gold earring

Horn pipe

Hook

Eyepatch

Parrot's brush

Pirate boot

Telescope

Pieces of eight

Horatio

Horatio is a sneaky pirate who would love to beat Sam to the treasure on Puzzle Island. He is lurking on almost every double page. Keep your eyes open!

Horatio

HELGA

Horace, Horatio's pet snake

Pink Elephants

Puzzle Island is the home of the only pink elephants in the world. There is at least one pink elephant hiding on every double page. How many can you spot?

Now turn the page to begin the adventure…

Sam sets off

Early one morning Sam's adventure began. He was off on his treasure hunt. He waved goodbye to his mum and his dad, his granny and his little sister, and set sail for Puzzle Island in his new red boat.

The sun was shining and the sea was blue. It was a perfect day to look for treasure. But Sam knew he had to keep a special watch out for Horatio, the sneaky pirate. He was sure to be somewhere near.

Can you see Horatio?

I feel sick.

5

Where is Puzzle Island?

Sam sailed and sailed, until he saw some strange islands ahead. Quickly he checked his sea chart.

"One of them must be Puzzle Island," he cried.

But which one was it? Sam remembered that Puzzle Island was the home of the only pink elephants in the world. If he could spot just one pink elephant, he would have found Puzzle Island.

Can you spot a pink elephant?

6

Remember to look out for Horatio, and a piece of pirate kit!

The first clue

Sam jumped off his boat, tripped and bumped his head on a large signpost. He was in luck! He had found his first clue.

Sam looked around. He saw lots of paths and lots of arrows. But where was the red and white stripy arrow that would start his treasure hunt?

Can you see it?

FIRST CLUE
Follow the
red and white
stripy arrow

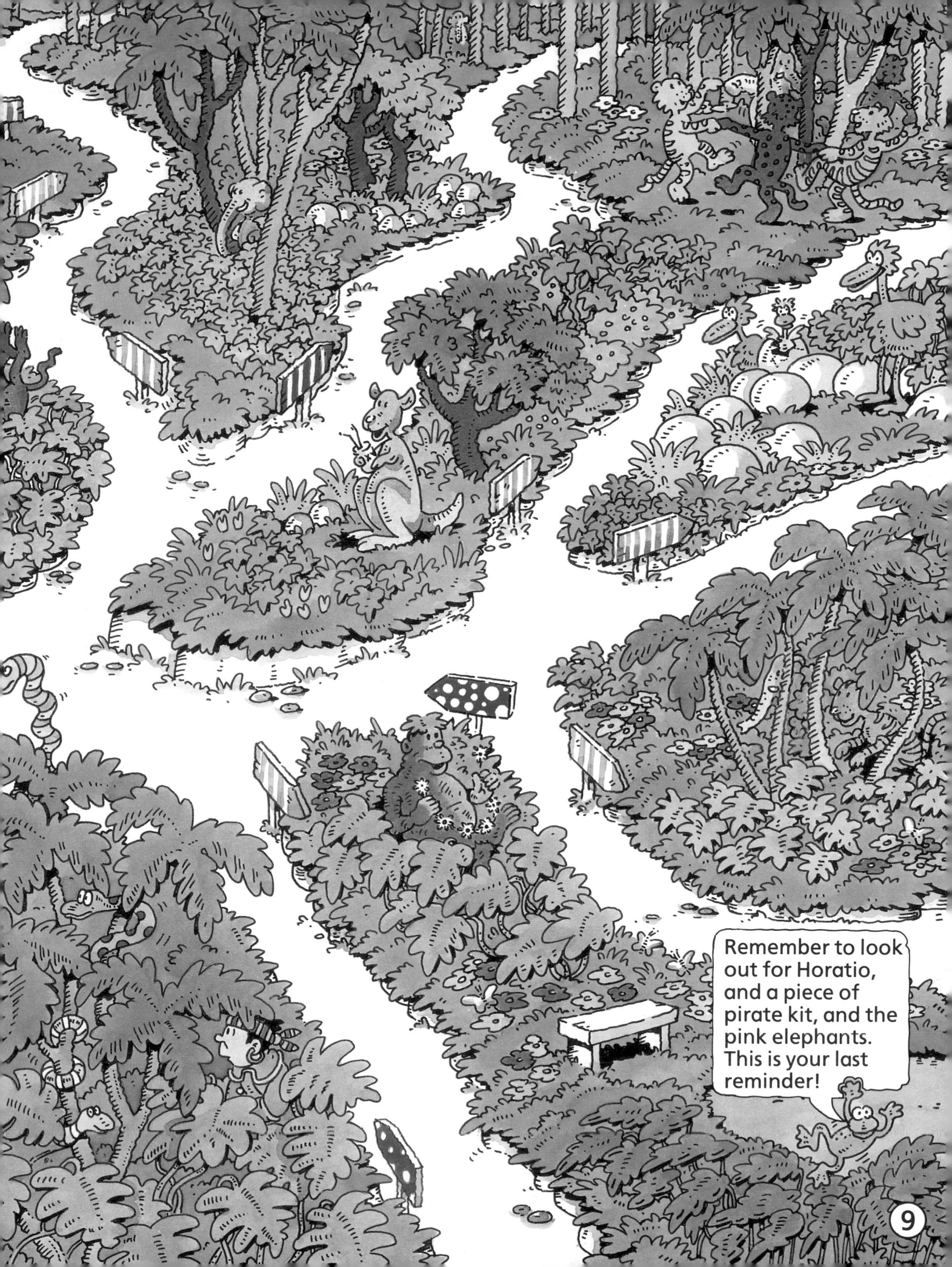

Remember to look out for Horatio, and a piece of pirate kit, and the pink elephants. This is your last reminder!

9

The leafy lake

Sam sped off down the path. He was so excited he almost fell – splash – into a big lake. He tried to run around it, but he couldn't squeeze past the prickly branches.

The lake was covered with lots of giant leaves. Maybe Sam could use them as stepping stones to hop across the lake? But some of the leaves were animals' nests, and some of the leaves had holes in them. He mustn't hop on any of these.

Can you find a way across the lake by hopping from one leaf to another?

NESTING SEASON
Do not disturb the baby animals

The safe bridge

Next he came to the edge of a high cliff. He gulped as he looked down. Far below he saw hungry crocodiles and strange animals, bubbling mud and whirling whirlpools.

Ten bridges crossed the gorge. Sam was about to step on to one of them when Percy squawked a warning. Sam looked again and saw that only one bridge was safe to cross.

Do you know which one it is?

Squawk!

Animal spotting

Safe on the other side, Sam saw a strange sight.
A man peered down at him from a tall tower.

   "I'm on a treasure trail and I don't know where
to go next," Sam called. "Can you help me?"

   "Yes, if you help me first," said the man. "I've
spotted all the animals in my animal spotting
book except for a lion, a tiger, a giraffe,
a monkey, a snake and a spotty dog. Find me the
animals and I'll show you the trail."

Can you spot all the animals?

The volcano maze

The old man told Sam to go to the red flag at the top of the volcano. There he would find something very useful. Sam looked at the maze of paths ahead of him. Would he ever make his way through them?

Can you find your way through the maze to the red flag at the top of the volcano?

Spot the difference

Go to the orchard

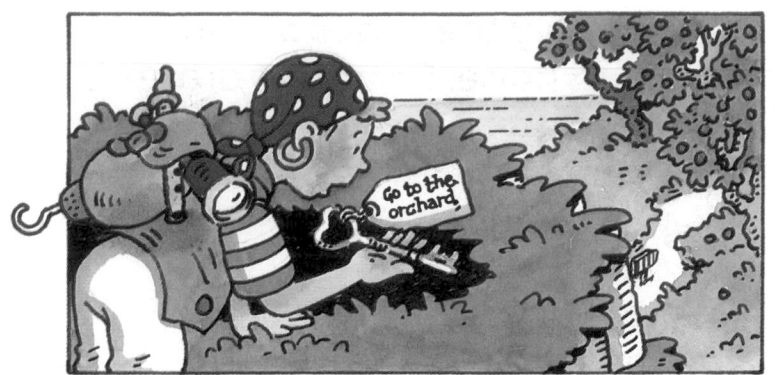

Sam followed the steep, winding path to the top of the volcano. There in the middle of the crater was a big silver key. It looked very useful, so Sam picked it up. Tied to it was a label which told him to go to the orchard. He put the key in his bag and set off at once.

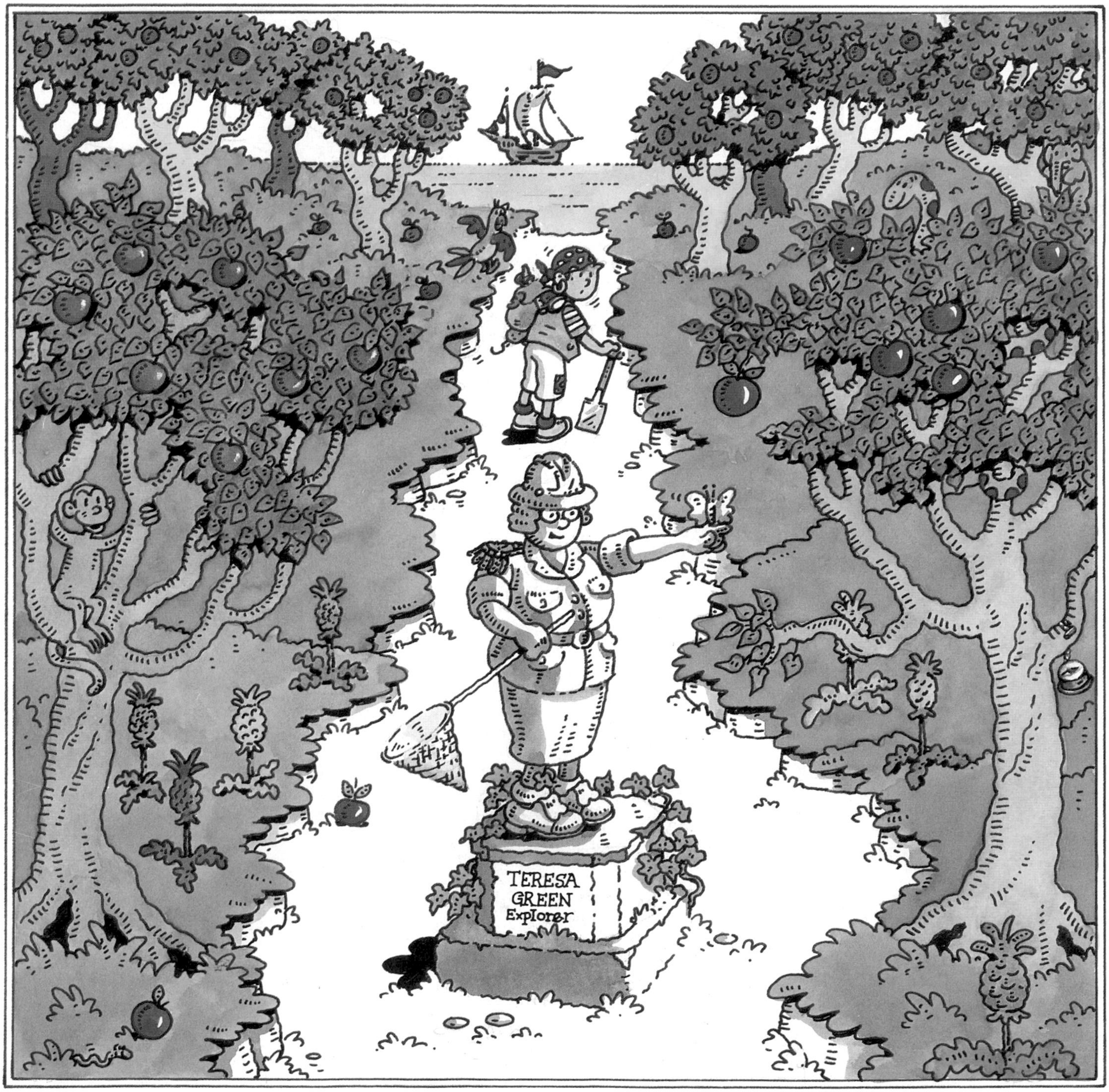
TERESA
GREEN
Explorer

When he reached the orchard, Sam thought he heard noises behind him. Was he being followed? Slowly he looked over his shoulder, but there was no one there.

"I hope I don't bump into Horatio," he shivered.

Suddenly there was a loud cracking noise. Sam spun around. How strange. He was sure there was someone else in the orchard, and several things looked different.

Can you spot the differences between the two pictures?

19

Find the twins

All of a sudden, Horatio leapt out from behind a tree. But before he could net poor Sam, he was startled by the sound of splashing and shouting. Nearby, children were playing on the beach.

"Which way to the treasure?" Horatio asked them gruffly.

Horatio looked very puzzled at the answers, but Sam smiled. He knew the way now.

Where should Sam go next?

Pyramid puzzle

Horatio sped off at once — towards the snake pit! Sam waited until he was out of sight and then ran to the pyramids. There were three of them, one yellow, one red and one blue.

Nailed to some trees, Sam saw four pieces of paper. Quickly he pulled them off and unrolled them. They were four maps of the area. But only one of them was right. This was the map that showed Sam where he would find the next clue.

You can see the maps on the next page. Which is the right map? Where is the next clue?

Map 1

Map 2

Map 3

Map 4

X marks the spot where the next clue is hidden.

Locked out!

There was a spiked wall all around the blue pyramid. It was much too high for Sam to climb, and the heavy gate was locked with a big padlock. Sam wondered what to do next. Was this the end of the trail?

24

Suddenly he had a brainwave. There was something in his back pack that would open the gate. Quickly he emptied his bag on the ground.

What can Sam use to open the gate?

The pirate's den

The lock opened with a click. Sam climbed the steps to a door in the pyramid and slowly pushed it open. He found himself in a pirate's den filled with all sorts of strange things.

There were six closed doors inside the den, and on each door there was a message and a picture. Five of the pictures showed places Sam had already been to on his journey around the island. But there was one picture he didn't recognize. This was where he had to go to next.

Which door should Sam go through?

Spies at the waterfall

Sam opened the door. He ran down the steps on the other side, through a door in the spiked wall he hadn't seen before, and along a path to the waterfall. On the ground was a cross. Was the treasure buried here?

Quickly he pulled out his spade and began to dig. Just then he heard rustling noises all around him. He was being watched, but he wasn't afraid. He knew the spies were friendly, because he had seen them all before.
How many people do you recognize?

The wonderful treasure!

Sam's spade hit something hard. It was the treasure chest! His friends cheered as Sam puffed and panted and heaved the heavy chest out of the ground. He opened the lid and gasped. Inside was the most wonderful treasure Sam had ever seen. There were glittering jewels and chocolate money, amazing toys and lots of toffees. Then Sam spotted the most important treasure of all. He was a real pirate at last!

Can you see what Sam has spotted?

Answers

Pages 4-5   Sam sets off

Here is Horatio.

Pages 6-7   Where is Puzzle Island?

Here is the pink elephant.

This is Puzzle Island.

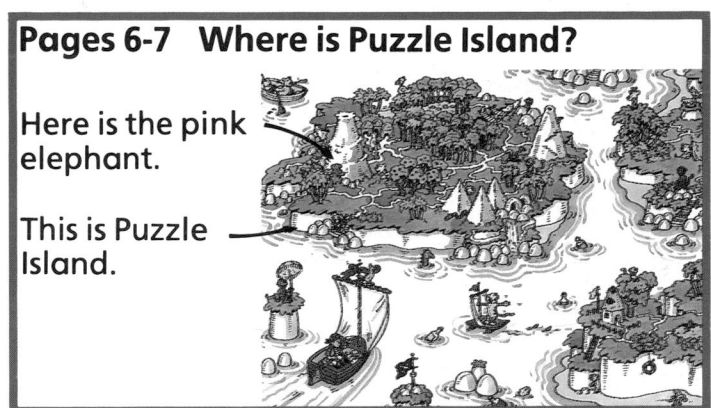

Pages 8-9
The first clue
Here is the red and white stripy arrow.

Pages 10-11
The leafy lake
The way across the lake is marked in red.

Pages 12-13
The safe bridge
This is the safe bridge.

Pages 14-15   Animal spotting
The animals are circled in red.

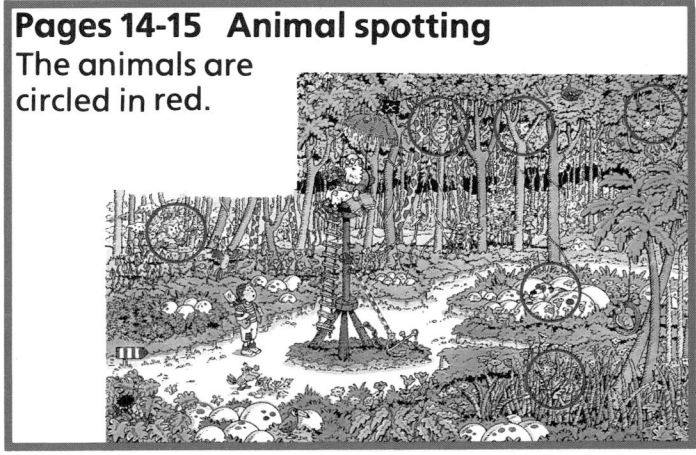

Pages 16-17   The volcano maze
The way to the red flag is marked in red.

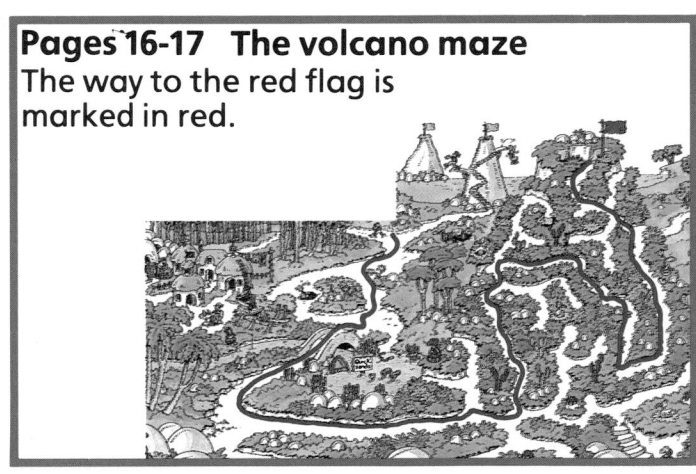

Pages 18-19
Spot the difference
The differences are circled in red.

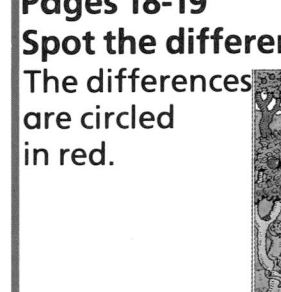

Pages 20-21
Find the twins
These are the identical twins.

Pages 22-23
Pyramid puzzle
This is the right map. The next clue is in the blue pyramid.

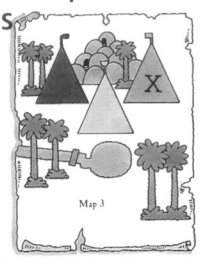

Pages 24-25
Locked out!
Sam can use the key he found on the volcano.

Pages 26-27
The pirate's den
Sam should go through this door.

Pages 28-29 Spies at the waterfall

You don't need an answer to this! Look back through the book and see if you can spot all the characters.

Page 30   The wonderful treasure!

Sam has spotted the skull and crossbones badge. Now he is a real pirate.

Did you spot everything?

Pink Elephants

Pirate Kit

Horatio

The chart below shows you how many pink elephants are hiding on each double page. You can also find out which piece of Sam's pirate kit is hidden on which double page.

Did you remember to look out for Horatio? He may be a sneaky pirate, but he's not as good at hiding as he thinks he is. Look back through the book again and see if you can find him.

Pages	Pink Elephants	Pirate Kit
4-5	Two	Boot
6-7	One	Grog bottle
8-9	Six	Telescope
10-11	Two	Earring
12-13	Two	Spare headscarf
14-15	Three	Hook
16-17	Three	Hornpipe
18-19	One	Compass
20-21	Two	Eyepatch
22-23	Three	Pieces of eight
24-25	Three	Parrot brush
26-27	Two	Cutlass
28-29	Two	Hat
30	Two	

First published in 1990 by Usborne Publishing Ltd, Usborne House, 83-85 Saffron Hill, London EC1N 8RT, England.

Copyright © 1990 Usborne Publishing Ltd.

The name Usborne and the device 🎈 are Trade Marks of Usborne Publishing Ltd.

Printed in Portugal.